J.C. Hulsey Books

TEXAS RANGER
BRANCH LOGAN
I WILL DEFEND WHAT'S MINE

P.L. THOMPSON

Cover Art by Michael Thomas
Cover design by J.C. Hulsey Books
Published by J.C. Hulsey Books
April 2021
10987654321

FOREWORD:

Branch Logan just got his butt piled in the dirt by a bucking horse. The captain rode up to the fence and without asking if he was hurt, said, "When yer thru wallowing around in the dirt, yer going to New Mexico."

******

In the year of eighteen hundred and eighty, Roger and Helen Bruster had moved to the Mora River Valley, several miles east, southeast of Watrous, New Mexico. They had bought the old Ortiz Land Grant, which consisted of nineteen hundred and twenty acres. Of that, right along the north river bank, a hundred and sixty acres were fenced, where a beautiful orchard and vegetable garden grew.

The main house was rock and adobe and a two-bedroom foreman's house sat well back under large cottonwood trees.

On this day, all the men were out on the east free range, rounding up cattle. Roger had just gotten back home to do evening chores when ten men came riding in.

The one in front said, "Bruster, this'll be the last time, you've got two days to get off this land, then my herd's comin thru."

Roger reached just inside the barn door and got his rifle. "Come ahead, I'll defend what's mine!"

"Yer wrong, this is free range and'll damn shor stay that'a way. I don't give ah damn about your Ortiz's land grant."

"Get!"

CHAPTER ONE

Late spring, Roger Bruster and five men took a load of vegetables into Watrous, and pulled the wagon to a stop in front of the grocery store. Roger went in saying hello to Mister Johnstone and his wife. "Thought I'd give you first chance on my first load of vegetables."

"My goodness yes! Mister Johnstone yanked his apron off and beat Roger back out to the wagon. His eyes were lit up and he said, "Folks sure have been waiting on this first load."

"I've got ten bushels, do you have room for them all?"

"I'll make room! When word spreads, I'll be out in two days. If you'll pull around back, we'll unload them in the store room."

"You didn't even ask my price."

"Roger, you're one man I'm not worried about overcharging. Whatever you say, I know will be a fair price."

"Then how does three dollars a bushel sound?"

"I was thinking more like four, but three is even better. That way I can pass the saving on to my customers. What kind of apple crop will you have this year?"

"Better than last year, I'm thinking. That river had plenty of water this year for irrigating."

"You will give me first chance?"

"Don't I always?"

They unloaded the wagon and pulled over to the hardware store. "You boys go on over to the saloon, I'll be there after a few minutes. We'll have time for one beer and still make it home by chore time. I meant to say I'll have time for one, you boys will have that first one down by the time I get there."

He walked in the store saying hello to Mister Tidwell. "Thought while I was in town I'd check and see if my wire and fence post got in yet."

"Not yet, that steel plant in Pueblo is having a run on wire. Yours will be in next Wednesday. Now about those fence post. I didn't know if you'd still want them at the price their asking."

"And how much is that?"

"A quarter each?"

"A quarter! No way in hell I'll pay that much. Any man I have can go down in those breaks and cut at least twenty a day. Naw, we'll forego fence post. My men will cut those. I'll see you Wednesday for the wire."

He walked out and got in the wagon driving down close to the saloon. He walked in and a beer was handed to him. Ward asked, "That wire come in?"

"Naw, it'll he in next Wednesday."

"Good, I'll be ready for another beer by then."

They drank their beers and headed out. The five men mounted horses. Roger climbed up on the wagon seat. Just as he had the reins in hand, up rode five men. One yelled, "Bruster, you got that fence tore down yet?"

"I do not and it's not coming down."

"I say it is, two weeks from now we'll be bringin' Mister Denton's herd right up the river to this here railroad."

"You'd better stay well upon that mesa. You'll not drive any herd across my land."

"I guess we'll see about that, now won't we?"

"You can tell Mister Denton I will defend what's mine."

"Do tell, do tell." They laughed and rode over, dismounting in front of the saloon.

Roger flipped the reins along the horse's backs and hit a long easy trot toward home. He could see trouble coming, bad trouble. Charles Denton acts like all of this country was still free open range. Well, by dang it ain't. Homesteads and small ranchers had deeds to their land and most of them had some fencing, gardens and fields had to be protected.

The next morning Ward, Roger's foreman and three men took two wagons, axes and saws and headed to the Mora River Canyon country to start cutting fence post.

Roger saddled up and rode back into Watrous. He bought ten boxes of .44.40 cartridges and six of forty-fives. Mister Moya asked if he was expecting a war. "Looks like it's coming, sure does. Mister Moya, do you think those nephews of yours would want a few week's work?"

"I'm sure they would. Do you want me to send them out?"

"Yes Sir, anytime they could get there will be fine."

He walked out and had just closed the flap on those saddlebags when Charles Denton and two of his men rode up. "Bruster, best you vacate this land pretty damn quick. That herd of mine'll be comin' thru there an' if that damn fence cuts any of um up you'll damn shor

pay."

"Mister Denton, that place was in the Ortiz family for

over a hundred years before he sold it to me. Now I've

told your help, do not try driving that herd across my

land. There's still plenty of open range you can cross, as

you've done for years."

"I'll be comin', I just hope the hell you don't cause

any trouble. If I have anything to do with it, all of this

country will always be open range, ever damn square

foot of it."

"There will be no trouble as long as you keep that

herd off my land. That orchard and garden supplies a

third of this town with fresh vegetables and apples."

"I don't give a damn about this town or yore orchard.

It's my herd I care about."

Roger looked at him. "Then we have nothing else to talk about."

He turned his horse to ride off when one of Denton's men yelled, "Don't you turn yore back on Charles, 'til he's done talkin'!" He pulled his pistol and fired a shot into the dirt ten feet in front of Roger's horse.

Roger turned back, "Do that again and I'll kill you!"

The man laughed and fired again. A split second later that pistol was shot from his hand. A cowboy was riding by on a big black horse and saw what was happening, and knew a killing was about to take place.

Denton and his other man started to grab pistols, but the cowboy said, "Don't be stupid an' dead. Be smart an' get the hell out'a here."

Denton looked at him. "You ain't heard the last of this Cowboy, an' neither have you Bruster!" They turned their horses and headed out of town.

Roger smiled saying, "Thanks Cowboy. I was out numbered and they knew it."

The cowboy asked, "What was that all about?"

"That was Mister Charles Denton, who thinks this whole country should be open range. He has a place east of me, over in broken country where the Canadian River runs into the Mora. His land is all free range and he holds onto it with guns."

"And you don't think this ought'a be free range?"

"No, not all of it. I sure don't think so as I own a small place east by southeast of here."

"Would it be anywhere close to the Ortiz place?"

"That is the place, I bought it from Ortiz."

"I didn't think he'd ever sell out."

"It seems you knew them."

"Yep, stayed a few nights out there when I's ridin'

thru this country years ago. Shor were nice folks."

Roger looked at him, "Do you have time for a cup of

coffee?"

"Yeah, that's what I was lookin' for, headed to that

café."

They rode over and tied up in front of the café.

Walking in, they shook hands, "Roger Bruster."

"Branch Logan."

As they sat, Roger asked, "Are you just riding thru?"

"Yeah, headed over to Las Vegas. Be there a couple

days er better, hope no more'n that, then head home."

"Where's home?"

"Midlothian Texas, southwest of Fort Worth."

"Now that is a fair piece. Just asking, are you any good with that forty-five?"

"I am, why do you ask?"

"It looks as if I'm headed for trouble with Denton, no way to avoid it. If you're not in a hurry, I sure might need help. I'll pay whatever you think it's worth, if you'd take the job."

"Thanks, I already have a job. I'm goin' to Las Vegas to testify in court against a couple fellers for killin' Jacob Gimbal. He had a little store in Mineral Wells, until they shot him for less than twenty dollars."

"You said maybe two days. If you think your boss down south could do without you for a couple weeks, I'll pay as much as a hundred dollars for any help you gave."

"I'm my own boss, got me ah small ranch I work when I'm not out doin' Texas Ranger work."

"Texas Ranger! What are you doing in New Mexico?"

"That feller they're gonna hang is from Texas. The judge don't hang him, I want to know when he's gettin' out of prison so I can be here an' take him back to Texas to hang."

"Then perhaps you can tell me where I can get the help I'll need. I know I'm in for a fight. The sheriff here in Watrous can't be of any help and the county sheriff out of Las Vegas won't come this far until after a few killings happen. I just don't want it to be me or any of my men."

"I'd say pull in close to home and protect it. You kill enough of um the others will back off."

"Yes, but if they destroy my garden and orchard, that would mean big trouble for me and my family."

"I've got to get on over to Las Vegas, that trial is due to happen tomorrow. I'll try to ride back over this'a way as soon as I can. At least before I head back to Texas. I'll ride out to yore place and might go on an' look that Denton feller up an' set him straight on ah few things."

"Anything you can do will be a big help. If you're not too late that is."

They parted with Branch riding for Las Vegas and Roger heading for home. About an hour later, Roger was on his property, but still a quarter mile from the house when his horse went down with a bullet in his neck.

Hitting the ground, Roger rolled and crawled back, getting his rifle from the scabbard and stayed behind his dead horse. Three or so hundred yards away, Denton yelled at his man. "Damn you, Les Howard! I thought you was a better shot than that! You killed the damn horse, not him!"

"I'll get him yet, y'all go on in case somebody shows up. That shot could'a been heard at the house er barns. 'Course somebody does show up, I'll kill them too."

"You'd damn shor better, then get on home. That round up is still goin' to take nigh on to two more weeks."

Roger heard as two horses took off in a run and almost stood, but remembered Denton had two men with him in town. He squirmed around where he could take a quick look over the dead horse's neck then ducked back out of sight.

He thought a moment, then said to himself. "I'm in a pickle, the men are down in the breaks cutting post.

Maybe if I lay here long enough, that old boy will think this horse fell on me and will come down to take a look."

He had the rifle hammer pulled back to full cock and waited and waited. He would hold his breath and listen for any sound. Up in the tree line, behind a few scattered boulders, Les was watching.

"I'm thinkin' he was hurt bad when that horse went down. Maybe he can't even move very much."

He stood and walked to his left twenty or so feet, watching the dead horse. "If he's alive, he'll think I'd come straight in. I'll circle all the way around…" A bullet took him down, dropping his rifle out of reach.

He caught himself, looking at that bullet hole. "Crap, now this'll make Charles even madder than he already is."

He hadn't realized he was right out in the open when Roger laid that rifle over the side of his saddle and pulled that trigger. Roger was now standing, walking forward not taking his eyes off the shooter.

Les reached with his left hand, trying for the fallen rifle. Roger fired his next shot at the hand, but hit the rifle, shattering it. Les jerked his hand back, and was trying for his pistol when he looked up seeing a rifle barrel sticking in his face.

Roger looked down, "Got you good. Can you stand?"

"Hell, I don't know."

"I'll take that pistol so I don't have to finish the job." He got the pistol then said, "I'll get your horse."

As he led it over, he looked down at the rifle and saw it wasn't worth picking up. Les asked, "What er you gonna do?"

"Try to get you up there in that saddle so I can get you to the house so Helen can dig for that slug."

"Why in the hell would you have her do that?"

"So maybe I won't have to dig a grave."

Ten minutes later Les was in the saddle and Roger was walking, leading the horse. Without looking back, Roger asked, "You have any money on you?"

"Well Yeah, why?"

"I just hope it's enough to pay for that horse you killed."

"I wadn't aimin' at the damn horse! I was aimin' at you."

"Not too good'a shot, are you?"

He led the horse over in front of the bunkhouse and helped Les down and inside. He let him sit on the edge of a bunk while he rolled out the mattress on one that wasn't already taken by one of the men.

He helped him over there and laid him back. "I'll walk up to the house and get my wife and hot water."

He walked in the house and his wife was cooking dinner. "Goodness, you were gone so long I just thought maybe you had gone out to check on the men."

"Is that kettle of water hot?"

"Yes."

"Get your doctoring kit, I have a wounded man in the bunkhouse. I'll take the water and a bottle of whiskey."

She walked from a back room, looking at everything she had in her hands. "I think this is everything."

As they walked toward the bunkhouse, she asked who was shot. "One of Denton's men took a shot at me and killed my horse. I shot him, but I think by the time you get thru with him he'll make it."

They walked in and she said, "Bring that lamp and stand over here and the wash pan."

She placed her kit and towels on the foot of the bunk, then pulled a chair away from the table and sat down. "I have to remove that bloody shirt." She started undoing buttons.

He looked at her. "You don't look like no doctor? You know what the hell yer doin'?"

"Watch your mouth! I could just let you lay here and die of lead poison."

Roger walked over with the water and handed Les the bottle of whiskey. "Suck on this a few swigs."

Helen cleaned off the blood while saying, "Two more inches to the right and I wouldn't have to be doing this."

Les asked, "Why not?"

"You'd be dead." She wadded up a washrag and said, "Open your mouth."

He did and she shoved that washrag in. "That's so you won't scream in my ear when I prob for that slug."

He damn near passed out from the pain, but she pulled the lead free, then quickly dabbed at that hole with a wet cloth. After a couple minutes she said, "This will hurt almost as much. I have to sew that hole up, then wipe on salve and bandage it. I'd say It will be a few days before you can sit a saddle."

Before the salve, she dabbed on just a bit of whiskey and he thought he was on fire. When she finished, she stood looking down at him. "I'll have Roger bring you some dinner after a bit, if I remembered to take it off the heat. If I didn't, it will be burnt."

Roger told him, "I'll get that horse taken care of, then bring your dinner."

He looked up at Roger. "Why are y'all doin' this?"

"Beats the hell out of me, we just don't like to see anyone suffer. I just hope the hell I don't have to kill you later on when you come back with Denton to try and wipe me out."

Late that afternoon around four, the men brought in two wagons loaded with fence post. Roger walked out, smiling. "Now by jacks that's quite a load. We'll take care of the teams and unload those tomorrow. Helen has on a big roast for supper and it'll be ready by the time chores are done.

As they removed the harnesses and opened the gate to the corral, Ward asked, "Who's horse is that? Yeah an' where's yours?"

"Mine's dead, while the other boys do chores, why don't we unsaddle one of y'alls and we'll ride up there and get my saddle and gear. I have two saddlebags full of cartridges it looks like we're going to need."

"Then you really think Denton is going to try and drive that herd right up the river?"

"Said he was going to, and I'd say he'll try. The fellow that shot my horse is in the bunkhouse. Helen took my slug out of him. He said he was trying for me, not my horse."

"Rotten shot, huh? 'Course you can replace the horse, we can't do without you."

They rode out, leading a horse. Ward asked, "Think they'll send somebody lookin' for that one?"

"I'd think that. He was pretty upset I got him instead of the other way around."

As they took the saddle off that dead horse, two of the men had walked into the bunkhouse. At seeing Les, one asked, "Who'n the hell are you?"

"You mean Bruster didn't tell you?"

"Naw he was talkin' to Ward, we was busy."

"I shot his horse, he shot me."

"The horse dead?"

"It is."

"Not a fair trade then, that was a good horse."

They said no more and put their things away, then went on out to help feed and do chores. One of them at last said, "Just like Roger, take care of that sucker. Not me, I'd not do it."

"Yeah, it's easy to see you ain't Roger."

CHAPTER TWO

Over the next ten days, five more wagon loads of post were brought in and stacked. "Ward, why don't y'all take both wagons and go on into Watrous and pick up the wire? As you have a beer, pick up another bottle of whiskey. We used that last one on Les."

"When'll he be fit to ride?"

"In a few minutes. I'll get his horse saddled and lead him over where he can just climb in the saddle."

The wagons pulled out, with four outriders. Roger saddled Les's horse and led it up front of the bunkhouse. Walking in he asked, "You feel up to riding today?"

"Yeah, you takin' me into the sheriff in Watrous?"

"No, I'm letting you ride for home."

"You are!"

"I am, just you let Denton know, I meant it when I said don't try to drive that herd across my land. I will defend what's mine."

Les got up by himself and walked out, left arm still in a sling. Reaching up with his right hand for the saddle horn, he pulled himself up. He looked down at Roger. "Thank the wife for me. She done a right good job. Can't figger you just lettin' me go."

Roger gave a half smile, "Think on it Les, it'll come to you one day."

He rode east, kicking the horse into a slow easy lope. He was doing some mighty heavy thinking. No man he knew of would have done what Roger did. He knew if it had been the other way around, Denton would have just put a bullet in his head.

Roger was in the bunkhouse rolling up the mattress. Then he walked to the house for a midmorning cup of coffee. Helen said, "I saw Les ride off. Think he'll be back?"

"Wouldn't doubt it. That's what he's paid to do. If my shot had killed him, I'd thought nothing about it. But wounded, helpless, naw, I'm not that kind'a man."

"Thank goodness you're not. I love you just the way you are. When will the fencing begin and where?"

"I want to build a water gap across the river first thing, then go from there."

"How in the world are you going to do that?"

"It's not as hard as you might think. We stretch a tight wire across the top. Then we'll tie wire around that and down to heavy logs a couple feet above the water.

Rain or spring runoff will just float those logs then they will just fall right back in place as the water lowers."

"I always knew I was married to a smart man. When do you think Denton will come with his herd?"

"It could be any day now, but we'll be ready. Tomorrow we'll have wire and fence up there and could hear cattle coming for a good way off."

She poured him another cup of coffee and herself one and sat across the table. "I wonder what happened to that Texas Ranger you spoke with."

"Yes, I was wondering that myself. He must have had things to do that was more pressing. But he did seem very interested in defusing our situation."

******

Right close to noon, Les rode up to Denton's place. One of the men saw him coming and called for Denton.

They were standing on the porch as he rode up and stopped. "Where in the hell have you been? I see you was shot."

"Yeah, Bruster got me instead of me gettin' him."

"I see you made it to a doc."

"Naw, his Misses took out the slug an' doctored me. I've been in their bunkhouse all this time."

"The hell you say! Why'd he let you go 'stead ah takin' you to the law?"

"Just so I could bring you a message. He said don't try bringin' that herd across his property. Mister Denton, I think the man will defend what's his."

"He shor's hell won't if we stampede that herd a few hundred yards 'fore we reach that property. It'll lay that orchard and garden flat. That wire damn shor won't stop no stampede."

"When'll we be doin' just that?"

"You won't. You won't be no damn good for a month. The rest of us'll start the drive three er four days from now. Them damn cows was hard gettin' out'a that rough country. We'd think we had um all, then come upon another small herd. I'll have Earl take care of yore horse. Come on in an' eat a bite."

"Naw, leave him saddled, I want to ride out an' look at that herd this afternoon."

"You up to that?"

"Oh yeah, that lady done ah good job. Good as any doctor."

After dinner, Les mounted and headed due east. Denton stood there watching and said to the man next to him. "By damn ol' Les is tougher than I ever thought he was."

"Yeah, wonder why Bruster done what he done?"

"Soft, plain melted butter. If it'd been Bruster an' I was the one that wounded him, I'd rode up an' put ah bullet in his head. You watch, we kill him an' ruin ever thing they've got, that wife of his'll have to pull out. Damn right, an' that'll be open range again. Hell, I'd most likely have to start use'n that place as a line shack, er move in there myself."

The man looked at him, and had his own thoughts about that.

Les watched over his shoulder, and as soon as he was out of sight, he kicked his horse out. A couple miles later he crossed the Mora River and turned west, not slowing. Just over two hours later he rode back in the yard at the Bruster Ranch. Roger was in the barn and walked out when he heard the horse.

"Well son of ah gun. He must have felt so bad he didn't think he could make it home." He whistled and waved.

Les turned his horse and rode over. "Need help getting down?"

"Naw, I made it all the way an' talked with Denton. He's gonna bring that herd in three er four days. He wants to wipe out ever thing you've got."

"We'll be ready for him, thanks for the warning."

"Yeah, but that ain't all. A couple hundred yards 'fore he gets to yore property, he's gonna stampede that herd, knowin' full well that fence won't stop um."

"Dad gum, I never thought of that. We'll just have to be a mile farther out and try to turn them before he can stampede them. I take it you'll not be riding with them."

"Naw, couldn't do it after what you an' yer wife done for me. I won't go agin him, but won't be ridin' for him no more."

He started to ride off toward Watrous, but stopped and turned his horse back. "Want'a know how I'd turn ah stampede?"

"I'm listening."

"A few sticks of dynamite. Split that herd an' make um run around you up on them mesas. It'll take Denton an' the boys a week just to round um up over half way to Watrous."

"Thanks Les, I mean it, thanks."

"Least I could do. Wish it wadn't gonna happen."

"What are you going to do?"

"Ride out, Las Vegas first, then where ever I can land a job."

"With you being in the shape you are, that will be a while. You need a few dollars to hold you over?"

He laughed, "Naw I still have plenty, thanks. Yer the dad gum'dest man I ever saw in my life. A feller does his damn'dest to kill you, an' you an' yore family takes care of him. Mister Bruster, good knowin' you an' good luck." He headed for Watrous in a long gentle lope. He would stay the night there and ride on into Las Vegas tomorrow. At one time he did have a couple friends there, maybe he'd try looking them up.

Right at half way to Watrous, he met the two Bruster wagons and stopped to talk. He told them everything that was about to happen. Ward said, "Thanks Les, I'll not forget it."

"Nor will I. Take no chances, they'll ever one be shootin' to kill. Oh, the stampede, Roger figgered out a way to stop it. He'll tell you all about it."

"Figgered a way to stop ah stampede! I don't believe it!"

Les smiled, turned his horse and headed on to town.

All the way to the ranch, Ward was trying to figure out how Roger was going to stop a few thousand head of stampeding cattle. "Can't be done, not with the few men we have. Ain't got much time to get more help."

Les made it to Watrous well before Ward and the men made it to the ranch. Ward was a mental mess by the time he got there. He left the wagon with the men, telling them to go ahead and take care of the horses. He walked in the barn where Roger had already started evening chores.

Roger looked up, "Get the wire?"

"Yeah, an' met Les on his way to town. What's this he said about you knowin' how to stop a stampede?"

"It was his idea, we use dynamite."

"Dynamite! Yes that'll work! I'll be dog, turned out alright you savin' his life after all."

"I'll go into town in the morning and get it and fuses. We'll have to have one or two men a couple miles or so east. When they see that herd's dust, they can beat it back here and we'll be ready within the hour."

"The first thing we'll have to do is take out them front outriders, then spread out. We'll have to keep throwin' dynamite until them cows get well away from comin' straight in an' out on them mesas. Best we also have men dismounted with rifles, cause them ol' boys will be tryin' to stop us."

An hour later over supper, they all talked. They knew who the best rifle shots were, they would have rifles in their hands instead of dynamite. "We have at least two days to really get set. You all know where those out cropping's of boulders are along both sides of the river. That's where our rifles will be. It's up high and there'll be very little chance of any of those men firing and hitting you from the back of a running horse."

The oldest man looked over at Roger. "You think this'll make him mad enough he'll just ride in here tryin' to wipe us all out. I mean after they round up that herd an' get it to the stockyards."

"That wouldn't surprise me one bit, but we know they won't get it done. We'll have cover, they'll be horseback."

******

As they sat talking, Les was in the saloon in Watrous with a bottle in front of him. He looked around at all the cowboys and farmers drinking, talking and having a good time. This was the first time in years he felt really lonely, sitting there drinking alone. "Why does Charles think the way he does? Those folks have more right to that land than he does his. They bought an' paid for it, he marked out what he wanted an' squatted, an' holds on to it with guns. I don't think he's ever tangled with anybody like Bruster. He just might get his butt kicked. Least he needs it kicked."

The bartender walked over, "Cowboy, you've been mumblin' to yore self for damn near ah hour. Don't you think you ought'a go eat a bite an' get to bed?"

Les looked up and smiled, "That's a great idea. Think I'll just do that, thanks." He got up and headed to the café, but turned and looked at his horse. "Bet yer hungry too."

He took his horse to the livery, then ate supper and went to bed.

The next morning, he was up early, without the headache he was sure he would have. He headed over to the café and the only other customer this early was a cowboy of forty-five or so.

That cowboy looked at him saying, "Damned if you don't look like you had a rough night."

"Sort'a, just not as bad as it could'a been. Stopped an' eat a bite. 'fore I went too far."

They were drinking coffee waiting on their meal when the cowboy said, "I'd say yer totin' ah bullet hole."

"Yeah, shor am an' the feller what done it took me home with him where his wife took out that slug."

"Oh, was an accident?"

"Naw, on purpose like after I missed him with ah shot an' killed his horse. He was a better shot than I was."

"Why was you shootin' at him?"

"My boss at the time told me to, yeah an' I was more'n willin' to do it. Shows how dumb a feller can be, huh?"

They ate and talked some more and the cowboy asked, "You goin' back an' try to finish the job?"

"Hell no! Not after him an' his wife saved my life an' doctored me like they did. I'd not made it, if it'd been anybody else that shot me. Anybody else would'a rode over an' put another slug in me er left me there to die. I'd bled out pretty quick he hadn't plugged that hole."

"You pay for the horse?"

"I did, er maybe he'd kept mine an' put me ah foot."

The cowboy stood, "Well Partner, I have to get on out to the Bruster Ranch…"

"Bruster! That's the feller that shot me, then took care of me. He's in for it though. Charles Denton is gettin' ready to stampede a few thousand head of cattle right up that river, right thru Bruster's place. I told him I'd get an' use dynamite to turn that herd. He does that, he's got ah chance."

"Then it sounds as if I'm not too late. He asked for my help a couple weeks ah go, but I got tied up."

Branch stepped from the café and had just untied his horse when a horse slid to a stop just feet away. "Ranger, I'm shor glad I caught you! I's afraid I'd have to ride all the way to Texas."

"What happened?"

"Ace Blocker grabbed my gun an' shot the sheriff. He knowed you'd be comin' for him so he sent me to get you. He made Sheriff Luna ride with him down to Romeroville where he said he'd be waitin' on you. You don't show up he'll kill the sheriff."

"Well I'll be a no good… Alright let's go."

Branch mounted, but looked east toward the Bruster Ranch. "Bruster, I just hope you know how to use…"

Roger was seen tying up in front of the hardware where he was going to get dynamite. Branch told the deputy. "That's a man I have to talk to for just a minute."

Roger was already in the store when Branch rode up. Going in, they said howdy, then Branch asked if he thought he could handle things until he got back. He told of a sheriff being held hostage and having to ride to Romeroville.

Roger said, "I think I have three days, but we'll be ready for them anytime after I get back home with twenty or so sticks of dynamite."

"I'll get back as quick as I can, don't know how long."

"It'll be rough, but I'm sure we'll make out."

Branch and the deputy headed west as Roger got his dynamite and fuse. He went back home and stopped by the house, as he saw none of the men around.

He called out for his wife. "Helen!"

She came to the door. "You wasn't gone long."

"No, there and back. Where's all the men?"

"Ward thought it best while they had time to push all our cattle back this way and west so they won't get mixed in with Denton's cattle."

"Good idea, I never thought of that. I'll be in the barn."

An hour later Roger had just started evening chores when ten men came riding in.

The one in front said, "Bruster, this is the last time, you have two days to get off this land, then my herd's comin thru."

Roger reached inside the barn door and got his rifle. "Come ahead, I'll defend what's mine!"

"Yer wrong, this is free range and'll damn shor stay that'a way. I don't give ah damn about you an' Ortiz's land grant."

"Get!"

Roger watched as they rode off. "Mister Charles Denton, you are in for one hell of a surprise, thanks to Les."

******

Just over three hours later, Branch and that Las Vegas deputy rode within a hundred yards of Romeroville. The deputy said, "There's their horses in front of the saloon."

"You ride on in and go tell Ace I'll be across the street."

The deputy rode in first, Branch eased his horse over by the water tank and stepped from the saddle, not taking his eyes off the saloon door. He walked across the street facing the door and pulled his forty-five. He rolled the cylinder twice, then let it slip back in the holster.

The deputy walked in the saloon and to a table where the sheriff and Ace Blocker sit. "You alright, Sheriff?"

"Yeah, yeah I'm alright."

Ace snapped, "That old man show up, er is he a damn coward?"

"He's waitin' across the street."

"The hell you say! What'd you have to do, pull ah gun on him to make him come an' save yore sheriff."

"Oh no, he was more than willin' to come."

Ace stood, "Deputy, you stick yore nose out the door 'fore I'm thru with that ol' man, I'll blow it off for you."

He lifted that pistol a time or two, making it lighter in the holster. Walking out, he had a mouthy grin on his face. "Old man, figgered if I didn't stop you now, you'd sneak ah round an' someday get me in the back."

"You've had a full day and night, I thought you'd be half way to Mexico by now."

"I don't run from old men."

"Like hell, you was runnin' when you left Texas."

"I wadn't runnin' from you Branch Logan! You damn well know I was runnin' from ten er twenty Texas Rangers. That many I can't handle. But you'll damn shor not be on my trail when I leave here."

"Are you goin' to talk me to death er try for your gun?"

He made his play, but never cleared the holster before the old man shot him dead with a bullet on the bridge of his nose. Branch walked over looking down at him, lying there flat of his back.

"Damn, I'm gonna have to have this gun checked. It's shootin' a good bit high. I was aimin' smack dab for the middle of his chest."

The deputy stepped out of the door. "You was not! I damn shor saw that barrel wadn't level."

"Yeah, but look at that, I messed up his whole face. How's the sheriff?"

"Good, the bartender wrapped his shoulder. He'll see the doc when we get back to Las Vegas."

"Let's go in and see if I can drink me a cold beer 'fore I head back to Watrous."

The sheriff was all wide eyed when he saw them walk in. "Branch., you got him!"

The deputy blurted out. "Got him ain't the half of it. Ace never even cleared leather. An' just think, we had to listen to his braggin' at how fast he was an' how many men he had out drawed. He was gonna shoot Branch, so he wouldn't foller him an' shoot him in the back."

He looked at Branch. "I can tell, you don't gotta shoot nobody in the back."

Branch asked, "Y'all want'a beer?"

An hour later they headed back for Las Vegas, with Ace's body draped across his saddle.

CHAPTER THREE

When they got to Las Vegas, the deputy took the sheriff to the doctor. Branch watered his horse and headed for Watrous. He knew it would be sundown by the time he got there.

Taking care of his horse, he then headed for the café. His gut was growling and he wanted it to stop. As he ate, he was thinking he sure needed to get on back home. To himself he was thinking, maybe he could ride out and talk to that Denton fellow and dodge a fight for Roger and his men.

Of course Branch didn't know Charles Denton. That man was living in the past and wanted all of this country to be open range and nothing short of losing one hell of a fight would change his mind. That or a bullet to the head.

After a good solid meal, he got a hotel room, then went for a beer. There wasn't over a half dozen men in there drinking and talking, but he wanted to find out all he could about Charles Denton.

He ordered his second beer and asked the bartender what he knew about Denton. The bartender smiled, "About as much as anybody I'd say, unless it would be the bartender up in Springer. That's where him and his men go most of the time. They only come here when they want to cause trouble."

"Have you heard he's about to give Roger Bruster a gob of it? Like running his herd right up the river."

"Heard that, but them thoughts of his has been going on for years. He'd try that even when old man Ortiz owned the place. Ortiz would have every relative from Albuquerque and Las Vegas lined out for two miles with rifles. He made damn sure Denton drove his herd well away from his land. I really think he's under estimated Roger Bruster. Now Denton has three times as many men, but Roger will protect his place. Them apple trees are stock from over hundred-year-old apple trees brought here from Spain. A herd of cattle could wipe them out in less than a half hour."

The next morning Branch headed for Bruster's and would ask him what he thought about a talk with Denton before it came to a showdown with cattle, dynamite and guns.

He rode up and four men and Roger had just hooked teams of horses to two wagons. Roger Smiled, "Step down, glad you made it."

They shook hands and Branch asked where the wagons were headed. "We'll place one sideways on each side of the river so my men will have cover. I thought three hundred yards east of my property would give us plenty of room to turn that herd."

Branch said, "I'd double that distance just to make sure. That herd will still have a long way to run gettin' around yore place, don't you think?"

"I guess you're right. We'll take the wagons on out now and unhitch the team and bring them back here so they don't get shot."

"How long do you think you'll have to wait?"

"I'd think sometime tomorrow is when they'll hit."

"What would you say I if rode on over to Denton's place an' have a heart-to-heart talk with him? Maybe I could persuade him to keep his cattle to the north of yore property. I'll not tell him what's waitin' if he don't."

"I don't think it will do any good. But if you want to try, go ahead, but I'd say it might get you shot."

"How far to his place?"

"Better than fifteen miles. Just ride straight east, don't follow the river as it angles more and more south. His place is where the Canadian runs into the Mora."

"Alright, I should be back by middle afternoon. I'm not back, you'll know you was right an' I got shot."

Branch rode out, kicking his horse into a long ground eating lope. He talked to his horse, saying, "Horse, let's me an' you hope he ain't as hard headed as ever body has told us. He has to realize he'll damn shor lose men. But again, maybe he don't give ah damn about that."

An hour and a half later, two men rode in front, blocking him. They both saw that Ranger's badge and one asked, "What's ah Texas Ranger doin' in New Mexico?"

"Right now, I'm on my way to talk with yore boss."

"Him an' Leo just rode in from the herd. We're roundin' up cattle fer ah drive down to the rail yards at Watrous."

"Yeah, heard somethin' about that."

They rode on down to the ranch house and Branch was impressed at how the place looked. Denton had been here a good while. They rode up to the barn and one of the men called out for Mister Denton.

A minute later two men walked out, one looked to be pushing seventy years old. He saw Branch's badge. "Texas Ranger, you lookin' for somebody on my place?"

"No Sir, hoping to avoid a showdown between you and Bruster."

"You can do that, tell him to pull down that damn fence an' pull out."

"He'll not do that, that's his home, bought an' paid for."

"Then I don't guess we have anything else to talk about. Tomorrow I start my drive and day after tomorrow I'll go straight thru his place."

"Damn, to avoid a fight, couldn't you just take yore herd to them stock pens over at Wagon Mound? It's a few miles farther, but real easy goin'."

"Not only no, but hell no. Them pens won't hold half my cattle. Springer is four days longer. No, I use the ones in Watrous, that's where I'm takin' um."

"I had to try avoiding blood-shed. You know he'll fight."

"So? I have him out numbered three to one."

"You know you'll lose men?"

"So will he."

"And that don't bother you none?"

"Hell no, why should it? My men know what they're paid to do an' by damn'll do it."

"I hope you pay them enough to die for you."

"Ranger yer stickin' yore nose where you have no authority. Best you butt out."

"Naw, think I'll stick ah round an' see the outcome. Don't think it'll be near what yer thinkin'."

Branch turned his horse to ride off, but Denton yelled after him. "So you'll know Ranger, I only hire the best guns!"

Branch stopped and turned around, "No need in bringin' yore own shovels, Bruster will bury yore dead."

He headed back to Bruster's, knowing this had been a worthless trip, but darn it, he had to try. Two days from now, men well die. Even before he got back to Bruster's, he was hungry and reached back in his saddlebags for some very stale jerky.

Eating jerky and drinking from his canteen, no need in trying, he just couldn't figure some men out. Willing to get men killed just to have his way.

He rode on and came upon the Bruster wagons, parked exactly where Roger said they would be. No one was around, so he rode on to the ranch. Men were sitting here and there cleaning their rifles and shoving ammunition in saddlebags.

Ward looked up, stood and walked over. "Let's get that horse took care of. Do any good?"

"Naw, he's a dab hard headed. He really thinks he can make a clean sweep of this place and lose very few men."

"I hope we prove him wrong."

"I think you will, I saw those wagons. You men will have cover, they won't an' I'd say if they hit any of yore men it will be an accident. Very few men can hit anything from the back of a runnin' horse with a pistol."

Ward smiled, "I think after a few sticks of that dynamite goes off, they'll be more interested in savin' a herd than shootin' at any of us. That herd is his only yearly income."

Two days later after morning chores were done and breakfast over, Helen handed Roger a large sack of food. "I'm sure none of you will be back for dinner. Just stay safe and do what you must. I'll see all of you this evening."

They all rode out to the wagons and dismounted, tying the horses on the off sides of the wagons so they wouldn't be hit by gunfire. The men were picked that would ride out a few hundred yards with the dynamite. Two men, plus Roger and Branch would have rifles to pick off the out riders that were leading the herd.

Right close to nine o'clock, two men came riding in and dismounted. "They're less than a mile back an' have the herd movin' right along. Only two of um are out front, maybe fifty yards, no more'n that."

"Alright men, let's go. Now I want the dynamite thrown, then get the hell back here behind the wagons just in case they do come after us instead of the herd."

They rode out and only had to wait a short while. The herd was seen coming and the out riders saw Roger and his men waiting. They turned their horses, riding wide around the herd and all the way back to Denton.

"Bruster has his men an's waitin' up there a few hundred yards. Saw six of um."

Denton smiled, "Six men damn shor ain't gonna stop this herd. Alright, let's run um an' don't slack off 'til we're plumb thru his place. Then we'll hold back an' let the herd stop an' go down to the river for ah drink ah water."

He and nine men that were there with him pulled their pistols and started firing. The cattle bolted, hitting a full run in only a few feet. The twelve out riders on both sides were taken by surprise and some had to get out of the way of the stampeding cattle.

They fell in behind with Denton and the other men, firing their pistols, yelling and hollering. The herd was now strung out for just under a quarter mile. With no riders seen with the herd, Roger and his men rode forward and lit the fuses.

When they threw the sticks of dynamite, the cattle never slowed, just turned left and right with more dynamite thrown. The men got rid of their last sticks, then turned their horses and raced back toward the wagons.

Denton couldn't believe his eyes. "They split the herd! They split the damn herd! Get after those cattle! I'll deal with Bruster later. Damn it ride! Get out front, slow um down er they'll run plumb to Watrous!"

The men, half riding left, the other half riding right by-passed the wagons by several hundred yards. No one from either side even got off a shot. As Roger and his men stood watching the herd, he smiled, "Ward, Branch, y'all was right about coming this far east. They will miss my place by close to a quarter mile."

Branch climbed into his saddle, looking down at Roger. "I'm thinkin' now, after that herd is safe, he'll come at you with guns."

"I'm thinking that also. Normally it would take a herd two days getting from here to the stock yards. If they can't stop the herd within two hours, they'll make it before dark."

"Then I'm thinkin' they'll hit the saloon tonight, an' hit you tomorrow. I also think yore place is easy to defend as Ortiz built it so he could defend it from Indians. I'm gonna ride on in and wait on um in the saloon."

"I think you'd better take help."

"Naw, they all know you an' yore men. Gunplay would start before talkin'. I'll not get in ah bind, if I can help it."

He rode out and didn't have the herd in sight for several miles. They were pushing it right along in between low hills, but away from the river. Branch rode south over low hills then back west. He made it to Watrous and ate a good meal, knowing it would still be hours before the herd got here. As he walked over to the saloon, he hoped Denton or his men didn't just go to shooting when they saw him. But still, with him already there, they just might think he'd been here all along.

Right at sundown he walked over to the café and ate supper. It was now getting dark and he was thinking maybe they stopped and bedded down the herd for the night. Just as he got back to the saloon, he stopped and listened and heard cattle bawling. "An hour from now they'll hit this saloon."

He went in and got a beer, then took a table with his back to a wall. It was well over an hour when men, tired and dirty walked in and bellied up to the bar."

Denton was the last to walk in and a drink was handed to him. He downed it in one swallow and asked for another.

They started looking around for tables, and cowboys got up and moved so they could take three tables together. Just before Denton sat down, he spotted Branch He walked over with a drink in his hand.

"You was right, that low life snake was waitin' on us. Damn near run my herd to death."

"I thought that's what you was goin' to do."

Denton looked at him, turned and pulled out a chair at one of the tables. Branch was just close enough to hear every word being spoken.

He and Roger had been right, they were going to hit just as morning chores were being done. That way none of the men should have rifles handy. Denton and his men would go in shooting, not giving anyone a chance to get to the bunkhouse and rifles. They would have the advantage of surprise and kill everyone of them, except the women.

Unseen, Branch got up and walked out the back door, then around front and climbed into his saddle. It was a good hour or better to Bruster's, but he had to let them know they'd be hit just before or right at sunup.

He rode up right at ten o'clock and saw as the last lamp was blown out in the house. He went to the door and knocked anyway, Roger had to know.

The lamp was re-lit and Roger carried it to the door. He was surprised to see Branch and asked him in.

"Naw, just needed to tell you Denton will hit early, sunup or before. I'll take care of my horse an' hit one of them bunks."

"Thanks, Branch We'll have an early breakfast."

It was still dark, not even an orange glow in the east as they ate breakfast and talked. Roger said, "You men know with that five-foot tall rock wall around the house, none of you have to show anything but your heads and rifles. Branch said they were to come in shooting, getting us on the run to get rifles. The first shot means they did come to kill, not talk. Open fire, pick your shots and make them count. It should all be over in less than five minutes. Branch, do you have anything to add?"

"Naw, you covered it all. I do think bein' as yer all cowboys, you'll try yore best not to hit a horse."

Ward asked, "We do have time to do chores, don't we?"

"Yes, Cooter, you get up in the barn loft. You can see them coming for a mile."

The sun was just breaking over the horizon, when they rode into sight. Cooter whistled and came out of that loft like his butt was on fire. Every man walked from the barn and thru the small gate into the yard and picked up rifles.

Roger said, "No one take chances, we know they can't get to us with that iron gate closed."

Denton and his men stopped several hundred yards out, looking everything over. One man said, "I don't see nobody."

"They're all in the barn doin' chores. We won't start shootin' 'til we get close an' when one of um comes from the barn, drop him. The others will make a run for the bunkhouse."

They rode in slow, so running horses wouldn't warn them. One of the men stopped his horse. "Damn it Charles, I smell a damn trap."

They all stopped their horses, less that fifty yards away from the front of the barn. Charles said, "Lefty, ride in there right slow an' see if you see anything."

"Oh no, not me by damn!"

"You'll damn well do as yer told er ride!"

"I'll ride, ain't goin' no closer."

"You dirty rotten coward! Get, damn you, get out'a my sight! Dale, get in there."

Dale rode in, looking everywhere and into the barn. He heard a rifle hammer brought to full cock and froze. A voice said, "If you want to live, unbuckle that gun belt and let it drop. Then dismount and walk to your right to a small gate."

He did exactly that with Charles asking, "Now what in the hell is he doing?"

One man said, "Maybe he's gonna check the house. Hell, everybody could be up yonder where we saw them wagons."

As Dale walked toward that gate, the voice had forgot to tell him to keep his hands down. Dale raised his hands and Charles yelled, "They've got him covered! Hit the damn ground an' open fire!"

They all jumped from their horses with a fellow asking, "What in the hell do we shoot at?"

"Shut up and watch Dale! No tellin' if they're all in the yard er not."

They watched, but saw no one except Dale as he lowered his arms. Charles said, "I think there's only one of um in there. We're walkin' in, keep yer damn eyes on that barn."

"But what about the one that's got Dale covered?"

"He's gotta stand up to shoot, kill him."

They stepped one small step at a time. Within a hundred feet or so that voice yelled, "You're everyone covered! Drop your guns and…"

Everyone of them ran for the barn. Roger said, "Take their legs from under them! Don't let them reach the barn."

Men stood opening fire and Denton's men started dropping. Denton and four men made it inside the barn. Denton was looking around like a trapped animal.

One of his men lay twenty yards away with a bullet in both legs. "Help me Charles! Damn it, at least drag me in there with y'all."

Denton yelled, "There ain't a damn thing I can do! I'm not dumb enough to go out there. We'll get clear an' come back for y'all, if we can an' yer not done for."

He turned to get farther back in the barn and see if they could get out back. That fellow that had called out, took a bead on his back and pulled the trigger. Denton went down. One of the men with Denton shot that one and hollered out, "Hollister got Denton! We're comin' out!"

Branch yelled, "Throw out them guns, then foller um!"

Three pistols were thrown out front and three men walked out, hands raised. Branch yelled again, "What about that forth man? Feller, one shot from you'll damn shor be yore last. The longer you wait, the more of y'all's men that have been shot will bled to death."

One of those men yelled, "Damn it Thad, throw that damn gun out! We're got good."

The pistol was thrown, then Thad followed. All of Roger's men walked out with rifles cocked and got pistols from those downed men. The four that had been in the barn and not wounded, was told to sit leaned back against the barn.

Roger and Branch walked in the barn and looked down at Denton, he wasn't moving. Roger kneeled down and saw his eyes were open. "You hear me Denton?"

"Yeah."

"One of your own men shot you."

"Yeah, in the back. You gonna finish me?"

"No, I'll send a rider into Watrous for the doctor and one to Fort Union. Both should be here within two hours. We'll make you and your men as comfortable as we can until then. Where you're shot, I'd say we don't move you. We'll roll you on your back and get something under your head. Your men will be brought in here also. My wife will get plenty of water heating, the doctors will need it."

Thad was one of those men sitting beside the barn wall and said, "Ranger, I think every bit of this was yore fault. You hadn't been here, we'd got it done an' killed ever body here. I think by damn I'll get another chance. Might be a little while, but by damn I'll be back."

Charles was resting comfortable, with his head on a saddle blanket and heard that. "Thad, let it go, we're done!"

"I'm not if I can talk this ranger into givin' me a gun. I'd like to blow his smart head clean off."

"Thad, I said drop it!"

"Yeah, all rangers are just like all law, cowards unless they have plenty of backin'. Ten rangers to get one man."

Branch whirled around and walked over right in front of him. "You've got a big mouth. You say one more damn word about the rangers and by damn I will give you a gun!"

"Now yer the mouth old man, all talk."

Branch jerked him to his feet. "Smart man, walk out there twenty feet… Hold it. Marv, take his pistol out there twenty-five feet er so an' an' lay it down, make sure it's loaded first. I don't want the hammer to fall on an empty chamber."

Inside the barn Denton asked, "Will you hold me up, I want to see this."

The pistol was on the ground and Branch said, "You pick it up and holster it. You try to turn and fire I'll back shoot you."

Thad laughed, "That'll be the day when a damn law man can best me in a fair fight. I guess when I kill you, all these fellers will gun me down."

"No, you'll be free to ride. Turn that gun on anyone else, they'll fill you full of holes."

Thad walked out and very slowly picked the gun up and let it slip into his holster, then turned smiling. "I thought you'd shoot me in the back, so you'd have a chance. I've killed ah lot of lawmen in my day, you'll be the first ranger."

Branch only said, "Mark, count to three an' get the hell out of the way. His slug could go wild."

On three, Branch shot him in the bend of the gun arm, then the left one and both legs before Thad fell to the ground screaming for help. Branch walked over. "I was just going to wound you one time until you went to braggin' about all the lawmen you killed. You'll never use a gun again and might not be able to sit a horse. Anything else you want to say about rangers?"

"Help me damn you, help me?"

"Naw, not right now, there's a lot of men in front of you that don't quite have the mouth you do."

He turned to Mark, "Mark, when them doctors get here, you make damn shor this un's last to be treated."

The army doctor got there first and was shown into the barn. He started to kneel beside the first man, but he said, "No Doc, take care of Charles first. He got it in the back."

Roger was right there and asked if the doctor wanted hot water. "I'll need it by the looks of things, but I want to look at this man first."

He rolled Charles over on his right side and looked. After just a few seconds he laid him back on his back. "Bend your left leg."

"I, I, by damn, it won't move."

"Try your right."

"Naw, don't move either. What does that mean Doc?"

"It means I won't touch you here. The operation you need can't be performed in a barn. If this gentleman has a wagon and a mattress, I'll have them drive you to the fort where you can be taken care of properly. One mishap, just one and you would never walk again and may be in a wheelchair for the rest of your life."

"Oh hell no Doc! Not that! Ain't there somethin' you can do?"

"I'm going to try, you just lie as still as you can. I'll start on these other men."

As the doctor moved on to the next man, Roger called Ward. "Get a team hitched to the wagon and put a mattress in back. I want this man well on his way to the fort a long time before the doctor is finished here."

As Ward walked out, Charles asked, "Why are you helpin' me?"

"If you'd been shot dead, I would have buried you. There's a chance for you to live and walk again, I'll help all I can."

Branch walked in. "It's done, I'm headed home."

They shook hands with Roger saying, thanks.